ANIMAL ALPHABET STORIES

A Treasury of Fun Alphabet Rhymes

ANIMAL ALPHABET STORIES

A Treasury of Fun Alphabet Rhymes

WRITTEN BY GRAHAM R. WIEMER

ILLUSTRATED BY JUDITH PFEIFFER

Publications International, Ltd.

CONTENTS

CONTENTS

Alphabet Song

A is for Alligator

A

A is for alligator.
He's asleep in a swamp.

A

A

He dreams of an airplane and apples to chomp.

A

ABCDEFGHIJKLM

He flies to Alaska
with an ant on his head.

A

A

A B C D E F G H I J K L M

A

The snow from above
almost covers their sled.

16

A

The alligator has an action-filled romp.

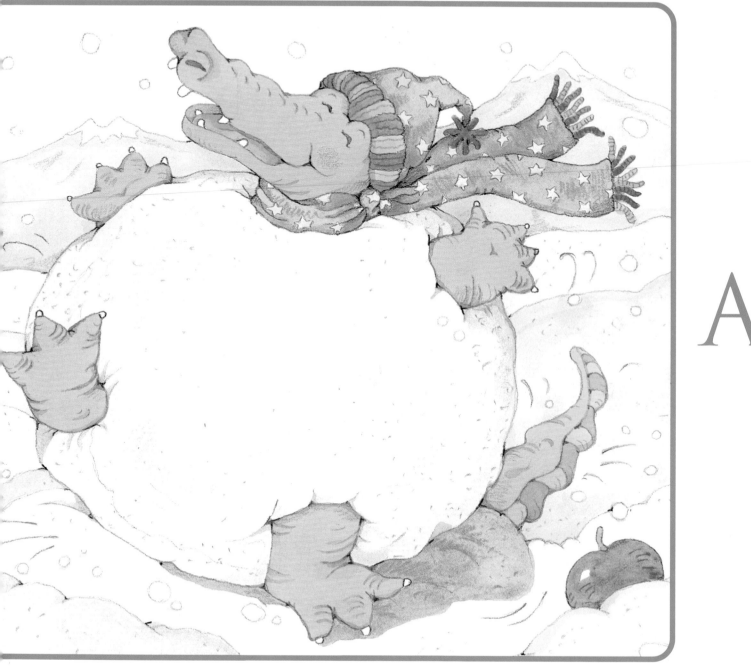

A

A

But alarm clocks go off,
and he's awake in the swamp!

B is for Bear

B

B

B is for bear.
She rides her bike to the beach.

B

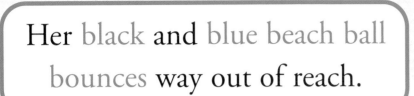

Her black and blue beach ball bounces way out of reach.

B

B

Because **it's her** birthday **she** buys **some** balloons.

B

B

B

She ties them to a boat
by some big, brown baboons.

B

The wind blows her hat,
with bright flowers on it.

B

B

The bear jumps way back.
There are bees in her bonnet!

C is for Camel

C

C

C is for camel.
He camps near a canyon.

C

Then he crosses a creek
with a cowboy companion.

C

A B C D E F G H I J K L M

C

They come to a circus.
Clowns serve cotton candy.

38

C

C

The cookies and cupcakes
and cherries taste dandy.

C

C

C

The cowboy's now chubby.
The camel can't run.

C

The comical critter
now has two humps, not one!

D is for Duck

D

D is for duck.
She draws, paints, and doodles.

D

D

D

Down by the pond
she sees dancing poodles.

D

A donkey drives by
in a dark red truck.

D

D

He drops off her ducklings,
who dive in some muck.

D

D

D

Their dresses get dirty,
and they haven't had dinner.

D

But mama has drawn up
a dish that's a winner!

E is for Elephant

E

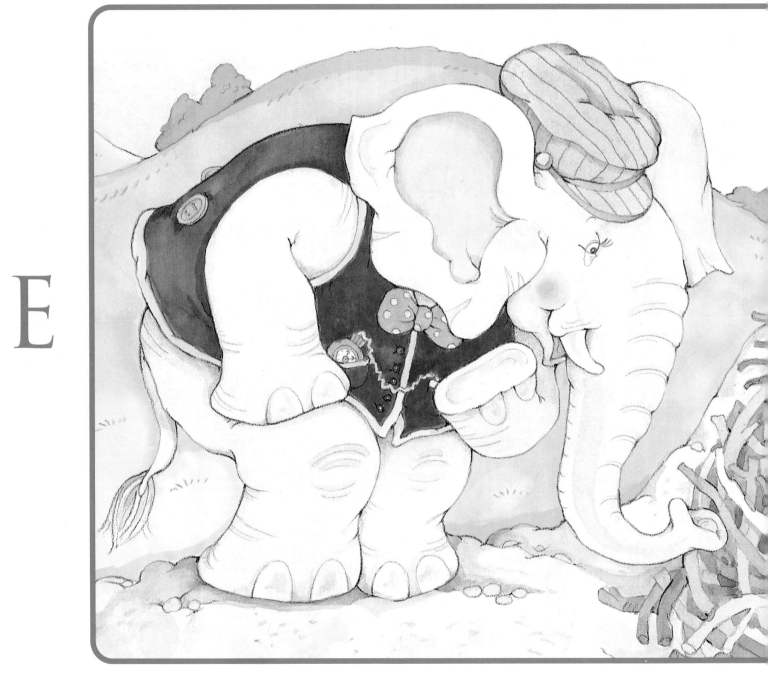

E is for elephant.
He finds eight small eggs.

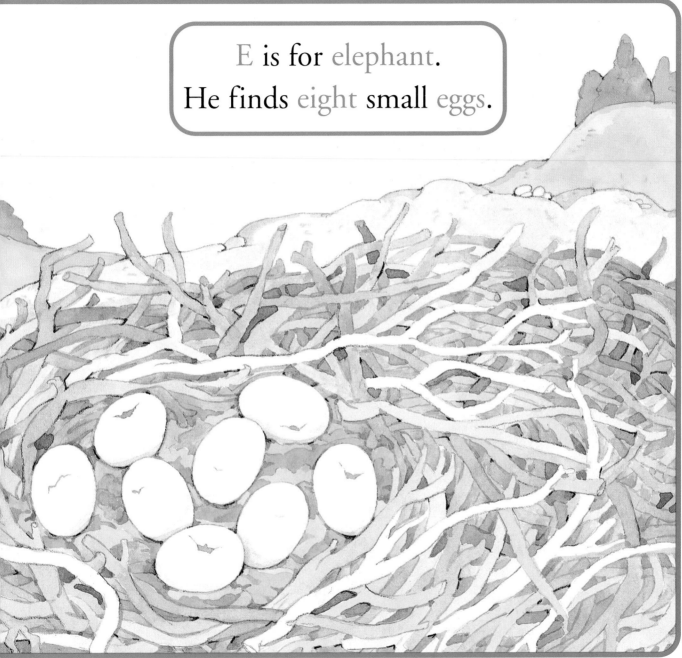

E

E

Out pop tiny eagles,
who escape through his legs.

E

E

He rides a train engine,
looking over the edge.

E

E

Then he finds every eagle near an extra-high ledge.

E

ABCDEFGHIJKLM

E

He helps them to eat,
even dries off their tears.

E

E

At the end of the evening he makes nests with his ears!

F is for Flamingo

F

F is for flamingo.
She flies to a farm.

F

F

She flops in a fountain
and feels safe from harm.

F

73

ABCDEFGHIJKLM

F

74

F

A fish sells her flowers.
They cost her five cents.

F

She sees a furry farmer
falling over a fence.

F

F

F

The fox rushes forward.
She flies for the towers.

The fountain is just for the furry farmer's showers!

F

G is for Giraffe

G

G is for giraffe.
He gets very good grades.

G

He's got to wear glasses,
but he looks great in shades.

G

G

G

He goes to the grocery.
A goat eats his glasses.

G

G

He wants to buy green beans
but grabs some molasses.

G

G

He guzzles the gallon.
It's sticky like gum.

G

G

Next time he buys groceries, Grandmother will come!

H is for Horse

H

H

H is for horse.
She hides near the hay.

H

A helicopter hovers
near a hill by the bay.

H

ABCDEFGHIJKLM

H

She puts on her helmet
and shoes on her hooves.

H

She hops a high hedge
but then hardly moves.

H

H

H

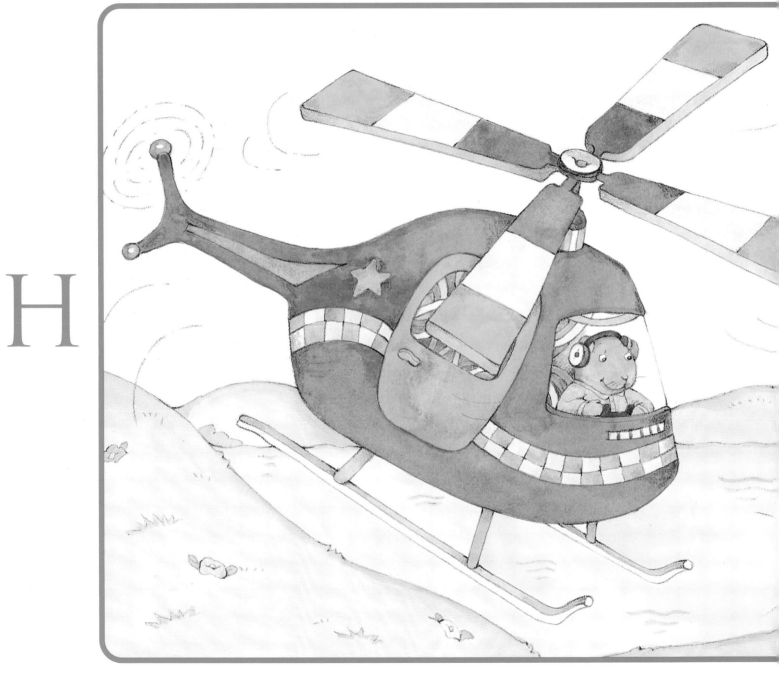

The copter heads closer.
It hurries and swoops.

H

A B C D E F G H I J K L M

H

A hamster has **brought** some new hula hoops!

I is for Iguana

I is for iguana.
He slides on the ice.

I

I

I

I

He falls on an igloo,
and inside are mice.

I

He's chilly and itchy.
He must get indoors.

I

I

The mice let him in.
The iguana just snores.

I

I

I

Then he rides on an iceberg.
"I've got an interesting scheme!"

I

"I bet where it's icy
I'll find lots of ice cream!"

J is for Jaguar

J

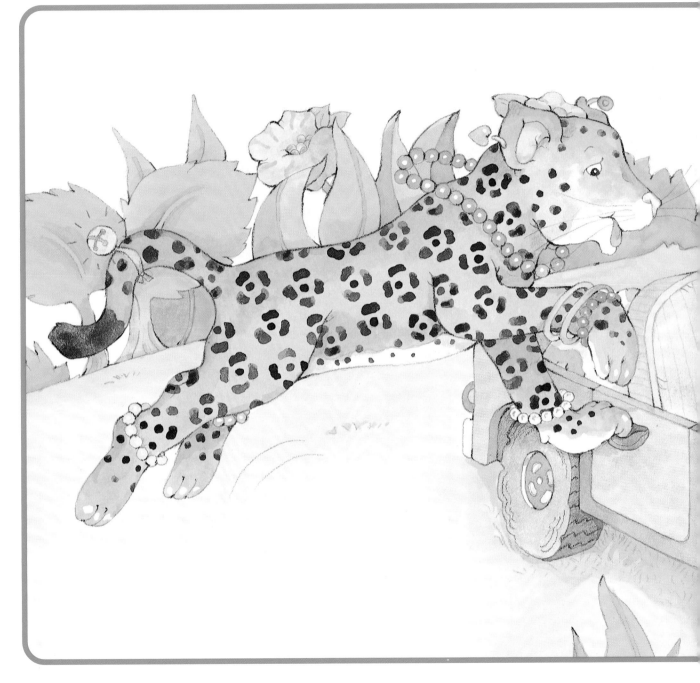

J is for jaguar.
She jumps in her jeep.

J

J

J

She passes a jockey
who juggles small sheep.

J

She wears jangly jewelry and listens to jazz.

J

J

She serves juice and jam
from some jars that she has.

J

J

J

And just when she puts on
her jacket and jeans,

J

The jockey jumps on juggling big jelly beans!

K is for Kangaroo

K

K is for kangaroo.
She's in kindergarten.

K

K

She plays a kazoo
that she keeps in a carton.

K

K

She kisses a king
who gives her a kite.

K

K

K

She ties on a key
while a kid holds on tight.

K

She finds a kind kitten
as she sits on a couch.

K

K

Out pops a koala
from her kangaroo pouch!

L is for Lobster

L

L is for lobster.
He lives in a lagoon.

L

L

Q. What did the Beach say to the Ocean?

A. Hi Tid...

He **likes** to learn letters and laugh **with** a loon.

L

L

He eats lettuce for lunch in a lodge made of logs.

L

L

L

He sees a large lady feeding long, little dogs.

L

Dinner Tonight

Special Surprise!

L

He looks near the lobby.
His heart leaps and flutters.

M is for Moose

M

M is for moose.
He's on a merry-go-round.

M

M

A magic wand appears on a mat on the ground.

M

M

M

He waves it and makes
a mini spaceship.

M

He takes a few mice
on his Milky Way trip.

M

M

M

His mom will get mad
if he's not back soon.

M

But he just has become
the first moose on the moon!

N is for Newt

N

N

N is for newt.
She finds a new boat.

N

She goes for a ride
with a nice nanny goat.

N

N

She nods off and naps on her neat sailing trip.

N

N

N

Then she heads to the north toward a big nearby ship.

N

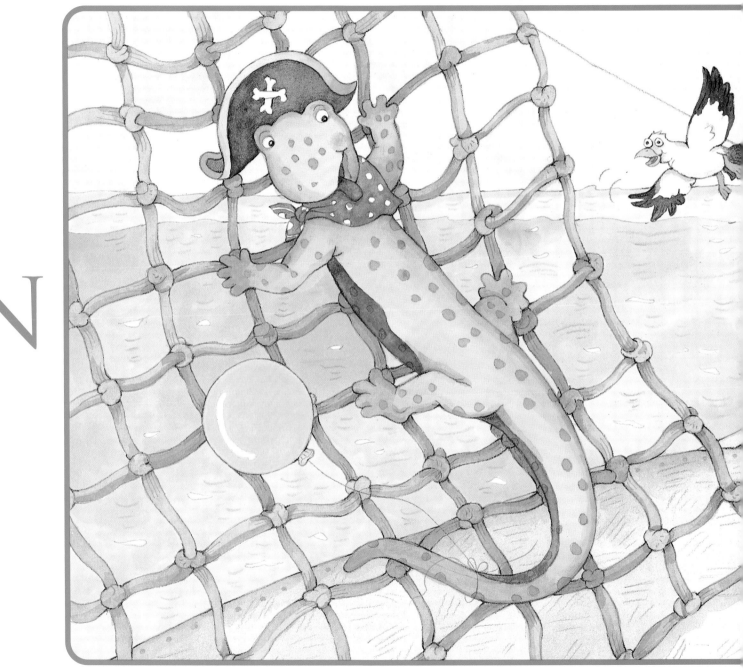

She climbs up a net.
She likes to act nutty.

N

N

She then joins the navy
with her nanny goat buddy!

O is for Owl

O

O is for owl.
She's out for a stroll.

O

O

She finds lots of oysters
that open like bowls.

O

O

O

Then out of the ocean
an octopus comes.

O

The owl plays an oboe while the octopus drums.

O

O

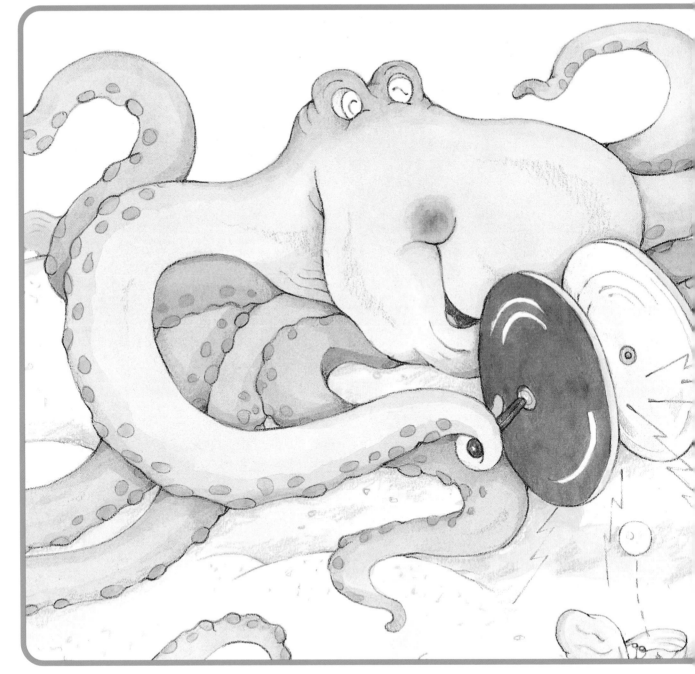

The octopus offers
to try something reckless.

O

A B C D E F G H I J K L M

O

He grabs all the pearls for the owl's brand-new necklace!

P is for Panda

P

P

P is for panda.
He plays peekaboo.

P

He peeks at a penguin
who lives in a shoe.

P

P

P

They make some pink popcorn,
then a bright purple batch.

P

P

There are piggyback rides
and a fun sing-along.

P

P

But the panda and penguin
won't stop playing Ping-Pong!

Q is for Quail

Q

Q is for quail.
She sleeps with a quilt.

Q

She quickly jumps up
and tries on a kilt.

Q

205

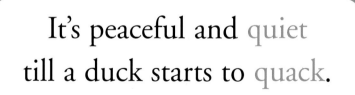

It's peaceful and quiet
till a duck starts to quack.

Q

Q

Q

She's late for a quiz,
but she grabs a quick snack.

Q

Q

The questions are easy.
She answers them all.

Q

ABCDEFGHIJKLM

Q

Her classmates decide she'll be queen of the ball!

R is for Rabbit

R

R is for rabbit.
He rakes by his rug.

R

R

Then right past his head
flies a red ladybug.

R

R

R

He runs off to chase her
as a rainbow appears.

ABCDEFGHIJKLM

R

R

A rock blocks the road.
It's as tall as his ears.

R

R

He rocks it and rolls it.
He's always been bold.

R

Right behind it the rabbit finds a real pot of gold!

S is for Snail

S

S is for snail.
She likes to play sports.

S

S

She **rides on** her surfboard
near a shark **who wears** shorts.

S

S

The sun shines on seashells,
on the sand and the turf.

S

231

S

S

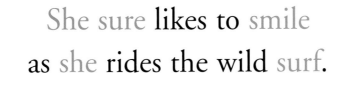

She sure likes to smile
as she rides the wild surf.

S

She swings **past a** sailboat.
She's **fast for a** snail.

S

S

She can go even faster
when she sits on a whale!

T is for Turtle

T

T is for turtle.
He's the talk of the town.

T

T

T

He buys a new top hat.
A turkey buys a crown.

T

T

They travel **by** taxi
toward **some** tattered
train tracks.

T

They're **searching** for treasure and they've **brought** two **backpacks.**

T

T

They **dig** **with** their tools
and they **make** tons **of noise.**

T

247

T

> Then they **find** that the treasure
> is a **trunk** full of toys!

U is for Unicorn

U

U

U is for unicorn.
She's under the stars.

U

Then up comes the sun
as she eats candy bars.

U

U

U

She unwraps each one
using hooves, nose, and teeth.

U

A squirrel grabs one
as he runs underneath.

U

U

Then umpteen umbrellas float up in the sky.

U

U

One hooks on her horn
and upward she flies!

V is for Vulture

V

V is for vulture.
He puts on his vest.

V

Then he buys a nice valentine for the girl he likes best.

V

V

V

V

He gathers some vegetables
that he puts in a vase.

V

He finds a nice veil
made of very fine lace.

V

V

V

Birds play violins
as he sits on a vine.

V

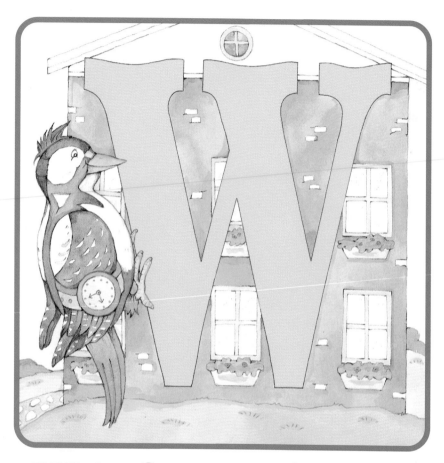

W is for Woodpecker

W

W is for woodpecker.
Her wings are her pillow.

W

W

She washes some windows
near a large weeping willow.

W

W

She's given a watch
by a very wise wizard.

W

W

It shows her it's time
for a white winter blizzard.

W

W

She pecks a wide hole
in the old wizard's hat.

W

W

There's a walrus inside
with a fuzzy wombat!

X is for Xig-Xag

X

X

X is for Xig-Xag.
He lives by the bay.

He goes to the doctor
and gets an X ray.

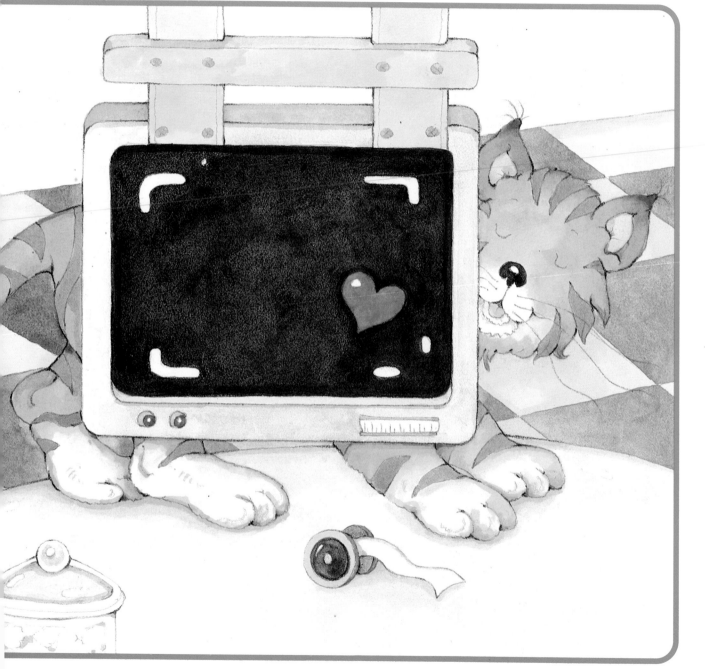

X

X

He looks at the picture
and sees all his bones.

X

X

Then he goes home and plays with his two xylophones.

X

X

Xig-Xag is careful
when he crosses big streets.

X

X

X marks the spot
where he keeps all his treats!

Y is for Yak

Y

Y is for yak.
She buys a new yo-yo.

Y

Y

It spins on bright yarn,
and she puts on a great show.

Y

Y

A young little duck
walks into the yard.

Y

Y

Y

Yes, he wants to play too.
Hide-and-seek's not too hard.

Y

The yak can't find the duck.
Then she hears a loud quack.

Y

Y

The yellow duck pops up
from the friendly yak's back!

Z is for Zebra

Z

Z

Z is for zebra.

He visits a zoo.

Z

His coat has a zipper
and the gate has one too.

Z

Z

He's in a hot zone
so he takes off his coat.

Z

Z

Then up zooms a monkey
and an odd billy goat.

Z

Z

Both have zero to do
so they paint some new stripes.

Z

Then they play tic-tac-toe.
These are real zany types!